This Faber book belongs to

For Effie and Tilly xx
P.J.

For Rose and Beth
L.H.

FABER & FABER has published children's books since 1929. Some of our very first publications included *Old Possum's Book of Practical Cats* by T. S. Eliot starring the now world-famous Macavity, and *The Iron Man* by Ted Hughes. Our catalogue at the time said that 'it is by reading such books that children learn the difference between the shoddy and the genuine'. We still believe in the power of reading to transform children's lives.

First published in the UK in 2018
First published in the USA in 2018
by Faber and Faber Limited
Bloomsbury House, 74–77 Great Russell Street,
London WC1B 3DA

Text copyright © Pip Jones, 2018
Illustration copyright © Laura Hughes, 2018

ISBN 978–0–571–32752–2

10 9 8 7 6 5 4 3 2 1

The moral rights of Pip Jones and Laura Hughes have been asserted.
A CIP record for this book is available from the British Library.

A FABER PICTURE BOOK

Quick, Barney, Run!

Written by
Pip Jones

Illustrated by
Laura Hughes

ff

FABER & FABER

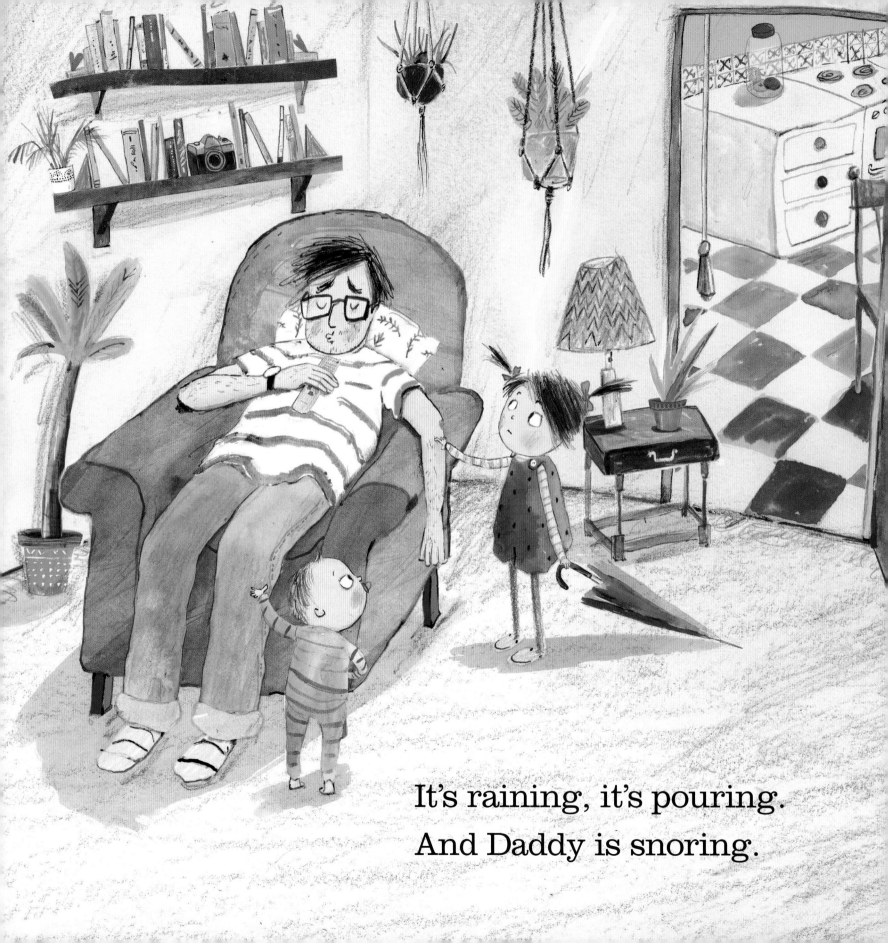

It's raining, it's pouring.
And Daddy is snoring.

Mummy is working.

Oh, EVERYTHING'S BORING.

There's *nothing* to do. What a dull, soggy day.
Not even my marmalade cat wants to play.

Well, I've had enough.
So come on, let's pack!

We're off to the jungle.
Not sure when we're back.

On with your goggles and seat belt.

Let's *fly*!

We'll zoom far away from this grumble-grey sky.

wwwwwwwwwm!

Bump! Bump!
We've landed.
Hey, look down below!
Right there!
That's the jungle.
Hurry, let's go!

But, *oh* . . .

How will we get down
these steep, scraggy slopes?
We need buckles and clips
and big knots in our ropes!

Ooh, it's gloomy in here.
Let's put on a light.
No, Barney, not *that* one!

That one's too bright.
Take the torch, tiptoe gently.
What will we see?

There's a beast up ahead . . .
Hurry up, follow me!

Oh! What a peculiar,
hairy old gibbon!
His fur's tufty, Barney.
Pass me some ribbon.

Tee hee! That's much better. The jungle is fun!

Uh-oh . . . He's waking! Quick, Barney!

RUN!

Wheeeeeee!

A bubble-gush river! Now what shall we do?

Let's both grab a paddle and use this canoe!

Whooooooooooosh . . .

Shhhh!
Look at the colourful bird
through the reeds,

tap-tap-tip-tapping
away at
her
seeds.

Perhaps we could try one. She's got such a lot.
I'll just stretch . . . nearly there . . .

Oops!

Maybe not!

You have to be brave now,
my little companion.
We don't have a choice.
We MUST cross this canyon.

Run as fast as you can,
till you reach solid ground.
Whatever you do, Barney Boo,
DON'T LOOK DOWN!

Eeeeeeeeeek!

WOWZERS! A tiger! Just look at its paws,
enormous great gnashers
and razor-sharp claws . . .

NO, BARNEY!

Don't poke its bum with a stick!

Too late. Now we're for it . . .

WAAAAAAHHHHH!